NIGHTMARE

BETHANY WINTERS

Copyright © 2022 by Bethany Winters

All rights reserved.

No part of this book may be reproduced in any form or by any electronic or mechanical means, including information storage and retrieval systems, without written permission from the author, except for the use of brief quotations in a book review.

This is a work of fiction. Names, characters, places and incidents are either the product of the author's imagination or are used fictitiously. Any resemblance to actual persons, living or dead, events, or locales is entirely coincidental.

Cover Design by Ria O'Donnell at Graphic Escapist

Edited by Zainab M. At Heart Full of Reads Editing Services

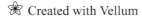 Created with Vellum

BLURB

VIOLET

He's spent the last seven months in prison for assaulting the guy who hit on me.
I've spent the last seven months wishing I could forget about him.
I ignored my parents and friends when they told me he was bad for me. I loved him in spite of his crazy. Maybe even because of it.
But when the cops dragged him away that night, I decided I needed to do whatever it takes to get over him. I ignored his calls, refused to visit him and pretended he didn't exist. I froze him out, hoping that would be enough to get him to leave me alone.
It wasn't enough.

ATTICUS

She's all I've thought about for months. The entire time I was locked up, I was out of my mind thinking about her alone out here without my protection. Not being able to see or speak to her almost killed me, but I survived. Barely.

She thinks ignoring me will get me to disappear, but she should know me better than that.

It's Joker Night—my first night of freedom—and I plan on making her pay for what she did. Right before I do whatever it takes to remind her how much she loves me. Living a life with me won't be easy. I know this. But living one without me just isn't in the cards for her.

I'm taking my girl back and keeping her this time.

This is a 21,000 word novella with themes some readers might find offensive. It is book 1 of the Joker Night series but can be read as a complete standalone.

PLAYLIST

Fire Up The Night by New Medicine
1x1 by Bring Me The Horizon & Nova Twins
Sick & Tired by Iann Dior, Machine Gun Kelly & Travis Barker
Popular Monster by Falling In Reverse
forget me too by Machine Gun Kelly & Halsey
Play with Fire by Sam Tinnesz & Yacht Money
deathwish by Stand Atlantic & nothing,nowhere.
NIGHTMARE! by Slush Puppy
Parasite Eve by Bring Me The Horizon
E-Girls Are Ruining My Life by Corpse
Follow You by Bring Me The Horizon
Gangsta by Kehlani
Centuries by Fall Out Boy

Listen on Amazon Music & Spotify

*"Therapist: You saw the red flags though, right?
Me: I thought it was a carnival."*

- Unknown

For Keiron <3

CHAPTER 1
ATTICUS

I'm going to kill her.

I mean, I won't *actually* kill her, because I'm not the type of crazy who likes to fuck dead girls, but I'll still wrap my hand around her little throat and squeeze until she admits she belongs to me.

It's been seven months, for fuck's sake.

For *seven months*, she wouldn't take my calls, reply to my letters, or come visit me. I was in prison, and she was out here doing fuck knows what. *Without me.*

Does she not know how crazy that made me? How I paced my cell every day and night and tore my fucking hair out, wondering who she was with and what she was doing while I was locked up in there?

Of course she fucking knows.

She knows me better than anyone.

Maybe that's why she left me.

Fuck that. It's *definitely* why she left me. But too bad for her; I don't give a shit whether she never wants to see my face again or not. I'm out now, and I'll do whatever it takes to make her mine again.

"Where to?" the cab driver at the train station asks, meeting my eyes in the rearview.

I give him the address and tip my chin at his center console. "Can I use your phone?"

"Something wrong with yours?" he asks, passing it back as he pulls away.

"I lost it," I tell him as I dial the number I memorized, pressing it to my ear once I hit the call button.

Technically, that's not a lie. I did lose it, along with my freedom the night I beat the shit out of Violet's *study partner* and set his dorm room on fire.

Fucking prick.

"Hello?"

"It's me."

"Atticus? What are you—" He stops talking, probably looking at his phone to check the number on the screen. "Wait, whose phone is this?"

"My cab driver's."

"You're in a *cab*?" He sounds baffled. "Dude, please tell me you didn't just break outta jail."

"I didn't just break outta jail," I say just to placate him, giving the driver my best smile when his eyes widen. "They let me out four hours ago."

"What? Why the fuck didn't you tell me that? I could have been there to pick you up."

"Because you would have told her I'm coming."

A short pause, and then he sighs, not even bothering to deny it.

I know he loves me like a brother, but he loves *her* like a sister and he's never tried to hide the fact that he thinks she's better off without me. He's a fucker for it, but I can't say I blame him. I'd probably tell her that too, if I was a better person.

"I take it you need a place to stay?"

I grin at that, shaking my head even though he can't see me.

I lived with Violet in an apartment off campus before I was locked up, and it's kind of cute that he thinks I want to live with *him* now. Like I won't be back in my own bed by Monday morning.

"I'm in Black Ridge, Phoenix. I'm going home."

"Atticus…" he warns, hesitating a moment before he decides to risk his life. "She's moved on. She doesn't want you anymore and you need to d—"

"If you tell me I need to *deal with it* one more time, I'll cut your tongue out and feed it to your mother."

"Jesus," he hisses, just as the cab driver looks up and makes a face at me. "The fuck, man?"

"Are you coming or not?" I mutter, feigning disinterest, but I'm secretly hoping he will.

Maybe just a little bit.

I don't *need* him or anything. I can get my girl back all by myself. But Joker Night has always been *our* thing—his, mine, Violet's, my twin sister's, and our two other best friends'—and it'll be way more fun if we're all there together.

"Yeah," he finally answers. "I'm coming."

CHAPTER 2
VIOLET

"Are you sure you wanna go tonight?" Andie asks, coming up behind me and wrapping her arms around my waist, dropping her chin on my shoulder.

I frown and look at her in the bathroom mirror above the sink. "Why wouldn't I wanna go?"

She doesn't respond because we both know the reason.

It won't be the same without him.

Every year on Founders' Day, we come home from college, go to the parade and smile for our parents like the good Founding Family children we are, and then we get ready for what we call Joker Night—the night me and my five best friends made up when we were *badass* high school freshmen, where we all wear Joker paint on our faces, get fucked up in the woods of our hometown, and let the other partygoers search for the Joker card we've hidden. Whoever finds it gets to ask one of us for a favor—one we can't say no to—but no one's ever found it, and hopefully they never will. I'm pretty sure some people think the card is just a myth by this point, whereas others take it super seriously and search all night.

We all know it's a stupid, childish tradition, but it's *our* tradition and we like it.

But *it won't be the same.*

I blink at myself, then clear my throat and look down at my chest. The old chain I'm wearing is long, the black, chunky cross pendant hidden between my breasts, but it still feels like a choker most of the time.

Andie's arms tighten around me, and I resist pulling the necklace out to run my fingers over it.

Don't think about him.

"Want me to finish that for you?" she asks, tipping her chin down at the paint on the counter.

I smile and turn around to let her do my face, trying and failing to listen as she talks to me about whatever drama her mom's cooked up lately. I barely hear a word she's saying, and I sure as shit can't stop thinking about him.

Atticus Lee—the boy who stole my heart six years ago and refuses to give it back.

He's toxic. Reckless. Dangerous.

Bad for me.

But even after seven months of silence and peace, he still manages to make noise inside my head. He invades every thought I have. He's a part of everything I do, of every decision I make.

When I open my eyes in the morning, it's him I think about when I'm lying alone in the bed he used to tie me up on.

When I go to get my coffee before class, it's him I think about when I give the good-looking barista my order, because it makes me think about the way he used to kiss me in front of him, because I was his and he made sure every guy knew about it.

And when I used my best friend's shower tonight, it was him I thought about while I was soaping my body, remembering the way I hooked my fingers over the glass door as he fucked me from behind on this very night three years ago.

"Are you even listening to me?"

"No," I admit, laughing at the face she makes.

"You could at least lie."

"Since when do I lie to you?"

She guides me out of the bathroom and into her childhood bedroom, placing me in front of the floor-length mirror so I can look at myself. Happy with my outfit and the creepy, bloodred slash across my cheeks and lips, I run my eyes over the length of my body. My long, dark brown hair and my toned, fishnet covered legs. My short black skirt and the black top that shows just a little too much cleavage. My tattooed arms and the piercings in my ears.

I study every scar and every flaw, and I can't help wondering what he'd say if he could see me now.

Would he tell me how much he hates this outfit on me, because it'd drive him wild with need, having to watch me wear it all night?

How long would it take him to sneak me away into the darkness, shove me down against the ground, and rip my shirt down the middle?

What would he say if he knew I still think about it…?

"Violet," Andie whispers, a little too soft for my liking. "Jesus, are you about to cry?"

"I don't *cry*."

"What are these, then?" she asks, touching the tears leaking from my eyes.

"Allergies."

"It's October."

"Maybe I'm allergic to your shitty makeup."

Her jaw drops, probably in outrage that I'd say such a thing. "My makeup is *not* shitty."

"Can we just pretend that it is?"

She snorts and wraps her arms around my shoulders, careful not to smudge our faces as she hugs me. I close my eyes and hug her back, mad at myself for acting like such a pussy, but this night is…special to me or some shit, so I'm cutting myself some slack.

"Better?"

"Not really."

"Ready to go make absolute fools of ourselves and drink all our problems away?"

"Fuck yes."

"Dɪᴅ sʜᴇ ᴛᴇxᴛ ʏᴏᴜ ʙᴀᴄᴋ ʏᴇᴛ?" Aɴᴅɪᴇ ᴀsᴋs, referring to Nova—our other best friend and my ex-boyfriend's twin sister. "She's ignoring me."

"She ignores everyone," I say as I pull my phone out, not surprised she's ignoring me too.

She's the biggest loner I've ever met, and we've been dragging her to parties by her hair—sometimes literally—since we were in high school. She's quiet, but not in a sweet way. All she has to do is look at someone with that glare of hers that says *I'll cut you*, and they'll walk the other way.

"I'm gonna go grab her," Andie decides, turning left onto her street. "You coming in?"

I nod, and she pulls up outside the house, hiding the new text message on her phone by shoving it into the center console. I raise a questioning brow at her—because that's the fourth time this has happened tonight—but she pretends not to notice.

Fine.

We climb out of her car and walk up the path toward the porch, both of us banging on the front door like crazy people until she answers.

"All right, all right!" her mom calls from inside, pulling the door open and shaking her head at us. "Damn Joker Night. Nova, get your butt down here!"

"Sorry, Mrs. Lee," Andie says sweetly. "She isn't answering her phone."

Michelle chuckles and waves her off like it's nothing, smiling sadly at me as she takes in my appearance. She's always been nice to me, having known me since I was a baby, and she felt bad for me when her son and I broke up—or when he went to jail and I ghosted him—but I know she thinks we're better apart than we are together.

"Violet, sweetheart. How are you holdi—"

Nova chooses that exact moment to appear behind her, staring at us over her mother's head without saying a word. It's kind of awkward and creepy, the way she's just standing there with her hair in her face, but that's Nova for you.

"Well then, you girls have fun," Michelle says cheerily, walking away toward the kitchen. "But not too much fun!"

"We will," Andie calls to her, looking confused as she thinks for a second. "I mean, we won't!"

Nova continues to stare at us, crossing her arms over her chest and tapping her stiletto covered foot. I don't worry that she'll ask me if I've talked to her brother yet, because I'm pretty sure she hates him just as much as she hates everyone else—probably even more. She and Atticus might be twins, but they don't have any type of special twin bond or anything. The only thing they have in common is their tendency to get mad at the drop of a hat. Other than that, they're two completely different people. He's loud and chaotic and up for anything, whereas she's none of those things. His hair is even darker than mine, whereas hers is so blonde it's almost white. I'm pretty sure she dyes it like that to make herself look nothing like him. It doesn't work all that well. I still see his golden-brown eyes every time I look into hers.

"What?" she bites out at me.

"Hello to you too, *friend*," Andie teases, raking her eyes over Nova's form. "Are you ready?"

"Yes."

Andie's smile falls, and she narrows her eyes, probably at her lack of Joker paint. "You're not ready."

The two of them have a silent stare off for about ten seconds, and then Andie rushes her inside and drags her upstairs, me following behind as they struggle and fight each other. I watch in amusement as Andie pins Nova to her own bed, straddles her waist, and takes out the makeup bag she brought with her to paint her face.

"You crazy bitch," Nova grits out, wiggling around beneath her.

"Hold still, sweetie."

"I hate both of you."

I roll my eyes and drop down on the bed next to her, chewing my lip as I stare at the door leading to the bathroom she and Atticus shared all through high school. She'd probably hate me a hell of a lot more if she knew how many times he fucked me on the counter in there.

Guy has a thing about bathrooms.

I push the thought away and look back at the girls, finding Andie cocking her head at me with a knowing look on her face. "You need to sto—"

"You wanna tell me about these secret messages you keep getting?" I cut in, because if she wants to play dirty, I can play dirty just as hard.

"They're not *secret messages*," she lies. "It's just my mother. High and broke, as usual."

"Your mother."

"Yes, my mother."

"Hmm."

"Hmm," she mocks me, flicking her curly blonde hair over her shoulder. "Talk to me when you can stop breaking your own heart over the boy you fucked in his sister's bathroo—Damn it, Nova, keep your mouth shut."

"*What*?!"

"How the hell do you know about that?" I ask at the same time, my cheeks heating when Nova hits me with that creepy death glare of hers.

"Vi, he used to make you scream like he was killing

you," Andie answers, grabbing Nova's head to keep her still. "It's kinda hard to ignore when you're sleeping in the next room."

"*I* was sleeping in the next room too," Nova points out, trying her best to speak with her mouth shut.

"Yeah, well. You sleep like the dead."

"That's true," I reason, rolling my lips when her eyes hit mine. "I'm sorry."

"Fuck off."

I laugh quietly, and Andie finishes her makeup, grinning like a maniac as she studies her handiwork. "Okay. *Now* you're ready."

WE LEAVE THE CAR ON THE STREET OPPOSITE THE GAS station, and then the three of us start walking once we've bought as much alcohol as we can carry. Andie leads the way, with me and Nova trailing behind her, cutting through the lowest part of the bush on the side of the road. We follow the beaten path into the woods, using the flashlights on our phones to see where we're going.

It's freezing tonight—October through February in Black Ridge is cold as shit—and Andie won't stop shivering and hugging her arms around her body. She hates the cold, whereas I love it. This is my favorite season. I'd live in fall forever if I could.

"Why do you never bring a jacket?" I ask, ducking under a low hanging tree branch.

"Because it would hide my killer outfit."

I nod with a light laugh, and we carry on walking. We know these woods like the backs of our hands, having been coming out here since we were old enough to sneak out, so it doesn't take us much effort to get to where we're going. By the time we get to the party spot just after ten, Nova's already ditched us and disappeared into thin air, probably through the huge crowd gathered around the small campfire. The flames keep us warm, but the alcohol and drugs will start to kick in soon and everyone will eventually spread out into the woods for the rest of the night, cold be damned.

People look over and clear the way for me and Andie as we walk, "Popular Monster" by Falling in Reverse playing loudly from the portable speaker on my left. Someone's already hung a bunch of Joker masks from the trees to make them look like severed heads—probably Trystan, because he loves this shit. Multicolored fairy lights are lit and strung up in the trees as well—we don't bring candles out here anymore, not after we almost burned this town to shit back in senior year—making it easy for me to recognize several familiar faces from college and our class from high school. The current high school students are here too, but we don't mind them. They're old enough to make their own mistakes, and it's not our job to tell these kids to fuck off home to their parents. We did worse when we were their age; shit so stupid I'm surprised we're all still alive.

"Yo, Violet!" Trystan shouts over the noise, walking over to meet us with that mischievous grin of his, tapping his fist against mine. "Looking fine, QB," he says to Andie, winking at her when she grits her teeth at him. "Where's your boyfriend?"

"Not here."

"Really?" He feigns surprise. "I'm shocked."

"Ha," she deadpans. "Fuck off, Tryst."

He smirks at her, but neither me or him bother saying anything else about it. I've learned it's better to keep my mouth shut when it comes to Deacon Wells. He's a college junior like the rest of us, smoking hot and loaded and smart as hell, but he's probably the biggest douchebag I've ever met. He treats Andie like shit because he thinks he's too good for her, but I think *she's* the one who's too good for *him*. I still can't figure out why she stays with him, and I'm not the only one. Her dad doesn't even like him, and he likes *everyone*. Even Atticus. Which is kind of a big deal because nobody likes Atticus. My own parents wouldn't even let him inside our house when we were dating in high school, and now that he's gone, they just love telling me *I told you so*. Constantly reminding me what a mistake it was for me to fall for him and that I should have gotten rid of him years ago.

Don't think about it.

Don't...

Fuck it, just don't think at all.

"I need a drink."

Trystan opens his mouth to say something to me, but Andie cuts him off with a hard glare, shaking her head as she pulls me away by my hand.

"But, Vi—"

"Shut up, Tryst."

"Fine," he calls after us, laughing as he heads toward a group of college girls a few feet away. "Don't say I didn't try to warn you, QB!"

Andie ignores him and grabs us a solo cup each from the plastic wrapped stack on the bar—which is just a filthy, folding wooden table filled with cheap beer—taking the bottle of tequila from me to pour us a shot each. She hands me mine, and I quickly chug it down, holding my empty cup out for her to give me another.

"Are you sure you wanna be here?" she asks again, waving the tequila at me. "Just say the word and we'll take this home and go to bed with a dirty audiobook. Fuck this party."

"Andie."

"Don't *Andie* me. I'm worried about you."

"Why?"

"*Why?*" she repeats, shrugging when I give her a look that says *just say what you wanna say and be done with it*. "All right. Because your smiles are fake as shit. You drink every night. You haven't seen your parents in *months*."

"I'm busy getting my degree."

"And you hardly ever show up to class anymore," she adds, completely disproving my point. "And when you do, you're either high or hungover. Mostly both."

"What happened to drinking all our problems away?" I repeat her words from less than an hour ago, desperately trying to change the subject.

"I just want you to be *you* again. Like before," she murmurs, pushing the knife in deeper. "I mean…I know your boyfriend was a crazy motherfucker but at least you were happy."

"Wow," I say. "Thanks, Andie."

"I'm sorry."

"It's okay," I tell her, even though it's not.

I know she's not trying to hurt me, but I'm getting really sick of talking about this. It's bad enough that he won't leave my head. I don't need to keep hashing it all out in real life over and over again.

"Holy fuck."

"What?" I mutter, not looking at her as I start to mix myself a vodka soda.

"*Vi.*"

I frown at the panic in her voice, lifting my head to find her staring at something behind me. I follow her eyes and look over my shoulder, my mouth agape when I realize what spooked her.

My traitorous heart leaps up to my throat, and it feels like I'm choking on it as he stares right into my eyes, smirking and shirtless and handing out pills to a group of guys just a few feet away from me.

Atticus.

CHAPTER 3
ATTICUS

Her pretty lips form the shape of my name, and I almost forget how badly I want to hurt her.

She looks fucking *stunning*, her dead straight, dark brown hair teasing her elbows, her tits damn near falling out of the black, cropped tank top she's wearing. Taking my time, I slowly move my eyes down to her navel, to the pale strip of bare skin just above her waistband, and then down to the sexy black leather skirt she's wearing. It's so short I bet you can see her little pink hole when she bends over.

Fuck.

I take my lip between my teeth when I get to the chunky heeled combat boots on her feet, those fucking fishnet tights she knows I love so much, and I promise myself right here and now I'm gonna rip those off her before the sun rises tomorrow.

She'll be a hot fucking mess by the time I'm done, just the way I like her.

Just then, her feet take a step backward as if she can read all the thoughts running through my head. I snap my eyes back up to her face, finding her pale blue ones filled with unshed tears as she stares at me like she's seen a ghost.

I'm not a ghost, baby.

Not yet, at least. The only way she'll ever get rid of me like that is if she takes a knife and shoves it through my chest.

She quickly turns around and gives me her back, and I toss the big bag of pills I'm holding to the random guy in front of me. "Hand these out," I tell him, slapping him on the back before I make my way through the crowd around me.

I catch up to my girl before she can run and lock my arm around her middle, pulling her back to my chest and dipping my head to press my nose into her hair. She's stiff against me, her breath hitching when I cup her pussy with my free hand, a quiet growl escaping me when I realize she's not wearing a thong beneath these tights.

I knew she wouldn't be.

"Atty..."

God. Hearing her say my name like that after so long is like a shot of heroin to my system.

I know she can feel how hard she's making me against her ass, and it's taking everything in me not to sink my teeth into her neck and piss all over her right here. To mark her as mine for all to see.

Because that's what she is.

"*Mine*," I whisper into her ear, closing my eyes at the soft little whimper leaving her mouth. "Fuck, baby girl. I missed you so much."

"Atty, don't do this."

Regaining my bearings, I wrap my fingers around her throat and walk her forward, not letting up when she struggles to get free.

"Did *you* miss *me*?" I grit out slowly, my teeth pressed against the side of her face.

She says nothing.

I tighten my grip on her throat, and she swallows, digging her pointy black nails into my wrist. The vicious little bitch is clawing at me hard enough to draw blood, but I don't care. I love the way she scratches me. I love *every* fucking thing about her, even when it hurts.

"Baby, answer the question."

"No," she wheezes out, struggling for breath.

"No, you didn't miss me, or no, you won't answer the question?"

More silence.

I lose patience and pick her up off the ground, holding her up by her waist and neck.

"Hey," Andie barks as she catches up to us, fisting her hands at her sides when I stop and raise a brow at her. "Atticus, what are you… How…?"

"Spit it out, little girl," I say when she continues to trip over her own words, shocked to see me here, no doubt. "We don't have all night."

"Don't call me that," she bites out, always so sensitive, this one. "And don't you dare hurt her," she adds, referring to Violet, I'm assuming.

"But she likes it when I make it hurt," I say, grinning as I take Violet's earlobe between my teeth, biting it and making her squeal. "Tell her, baby."

"Vi?" Andie asks, ignoring me now. "What do I do?"

Those tears I saw in Violet's eyes before finally fall, and she lets out a choking sound as she curls in on herself and clutches my hand to her face, reaching up with the other one to run her fingers through my hair. She's still got her back to me, but she's clinging to me as if she's afraid I'm about to disappear into thin air any second now, and it's breaking my fucking heart.

Andie's eyes soften as she watches her best friend fall apart, and then she nods and tips her chin at me, silently telling me to go put her back together. She offers me a bottle of tequila, and I let go of Violet's face to take it from her, holding it between my fingers as I carry Violet away from all the nosy fuckers staring at us. They're smart enough not to look at her from the neck down, because if they did that, she'd be swallowing their dried-up blood later when I'm shoving my fingers down her throat.

The music fades the further I walk, and I can barely

hear it anymore as I find us a private spot in the middle of the woods. I set Violet down on her feet and lean her back against a tree, crowding her space and brushing her soft hair behind her ears.

"Violet," I whisper, running my thumbs over the red paint on her lips, smearing it up over her tear-stained cheeks. "Don't cry, pretty girl. I'm here now."

"Stop it," she chokes out, smacking my hands away from her face.

"Vi—"

"*No*, Atty. I can't do this right now."

"No?" I ask, smiling a little at the fire returning to her eyes. "Why not?"

"Why are you here?"

"This is my party too, remember?" My eyes take in the necklace she's wearing—*my* necklace—and I pull it out of her top, wrapping it around my fist.

"I meant *how* are you here? When did you get out?"

"Today," I tell her, shaking my head when her nostrils flare as if she thinks she's been played by her own friends. "No one knew I was coming. Not even Phoenix. I wanted to surprise you."

She inhales deeply, and I use the chain to pull her into me and lick her bottom lip, locking my jaw when she slaps me across the face hard enough to leave a mark.

"If anyone gets to be mad here, it's *me*." I wrap my hand around her throat again, forcing her eyes up to meet mine. "Seven months. *Seven* fucking *months*, Violet. You almost killed me."

"You deserved it."

"You little bitch."

She slaps me again, and I snatch her wrists, pinning them to the tree above her head.

"Let me go."

"Not until you kiss me."

"Get fucked."

I cock my head and shove her legs apart with my knee, pushing my hips into hers, enjoying the way her lips part when I grind my dick on her pussy.

"Kiss me."

"No."

"Tell me you missed me."

"No."

Getting real sick of that word, I hold her wrists up with one hand and take her jaw, holding her head still and pressing my forehead against hers.

Her eyes are wide open, and she's staring at me again, studying the white paint covering the entire right side of my face, the black smudged around my eye, and the creepy red smile slashed across my mouth that matches hers.

"Tell me you love me."

"I don't," she rasps. "I stopped a long time ago."

I blink at that, pulling back a little. "You're lying."

"You think so?" She smirks, catching me off guard,

and it's enough to distract me from seeing her knee coming up and hitting me in the balls.

"Fucking cunt," I growl, not at her—I'd never call her that—but at the burning pain in my dick.

I drop to my knees and cup my groin, my mouth hanging open as I try to pull some air into my lungs. Somehow managing not to puke up my intestines, I look up and search for Violet, but all I see is her back as she walks away from me.

"Violet!"

CHAPTER 4
VIOLET

I CAN STILL HEAR HIM CALLING MY NAME. MY HEART IS racing, and I can't keep up with the thoughts running rampant through my head.

He's back.

He's really back and he's come for me.

I don't know how I feel about that.

I was supposed to have more time, more notice to prepare myself, to *not* be blindsided and carried away like a child in front of almost everyone we know.

Before tonight, I hadn't planned what I'd do when this day finally came. I wasn't ready to think about it yet, and now that it's happening, I don't know how the fuck I'm supposed to deal with him. Hitting him in the dick probably wasn't a good start.

After I did that and walked away, I found my way to this small, abandoned cabin about a half a mile from where we were before. Now I'm sitting on the cracked front steps, remembering the time he bent me over in this very spot and fucked me while the rest of our friends partied inside.

I should have gone somewhere else. Anywhere in these woods would have been better than this place, but maybe I was hoping he'd find me.

I hear him call my name again, and a sick little thrill rushes through me when I realize he's getting close. Knowing it won't be long now, I pull out the joint I stashed in the side of my boot and burn the tip with the lighter I found in Atticus's hoodie the morning after he was arrested. No one knows I carry it around with me everywhere I go, not even Andie. Or that I still sleep wearing his t-shirts and read his letters again and again when I can't sleep.

Those are my little secrets.

"That was mean."

"You used to like me mean," I reply, looking down at the ground as I blow my smoke out.

"I still do." He steps closer until his hips are right in front of my face, fisting his dick through his jeans to show me. "It's hard again now."

I wet my dry lips and find the courage to look up at him, smiling despite myself when he looks down at me and takes a shot of tequila right from the bottle. I hold the joint up and trade it for the alcohol, my throat burning as I take a drink. He's still watching me as he takes a hit, a white cloud of smoke drifting out of his full lips as he exhales.

I wish I could say I forgot how hot he is, but I can't. I could never forget a damn thing about him, no matter how hard I forced myself to try.

His tanned chest and abs are just as cut as they were before, maybe even more. His dark hair is a little longer and messier on top, like he's been running his fingers through it for months and now it's just stuck that way. His t-shirt is tucked into the back pocket of the loose, ripped jeans he's wearing. And those stupid, intense brown eyes of his…

We swap again, and he drops down on the step below me, putting his ass between my legs and sitting back against my inner thighs. I don't stop him, but I don't touch him either, leaning back on my hand as I smoke my joint in silence.

"Wanna play a game?" he asks after a minute, tipping his head back to look at me upside down.

"I'm sick of your games, Atty."

"Liar," he accuses. "Truth or dare?"

I roll my eyes and pass him the joint. "Dare."

He chuckles at that, not seeming mad that I didn't pick truth. "I dare you to kiss me."

I sigh and yank his head back by his hair, making him grunt, but he doesn't complain. I lean forward, but just as my lips are about to touch his, he turns his face away and taps his index finger against his neck.

"Here?" I ask, resting my mouth against the spot.

"Here," he echoes, moaning quietly when I run my tongue over his pulse. He arches his back and squeezes my ankles. "Fuck, I love you so much."

My heart somersaults inside my chest, like his own personal cheerleader, and I push him away before I do something stupid, like tell him…

No.

Stop it, Violet.

"Truth or dare?" I ask, clearing my throat when I hear how raspy my voice sounds.

"Truth."

Fucker.

I was hoping he'd pick dare so I could dare him to walk away from me, but it looks like he's playing just as dirty as I am.

"Who told you about Jared?"

"Phoenix," he answers, his eyes darkening at the mention of my old study partner. "He heard Jared the night he told you he was in love with you."

I remember that night. Jared turned up at the party we were at, got so drunk he could barely stand up straight, made his declaration while Atticus was playing pool with the boys in the other room, and then leaned in and tried to kiss me. I shoved his ass away and told him it would never happen, and I thought that would be the end of it. But not even forty-eight hours later, Jared's dorm room was burning, he was on the way to the hospital with a bloody face and a broken wrist, and my boyfriend was on his way to jail.

"Why didn't *you* tell me?" he asks, pulling me back from the memory.

"And if I had?" I hedge. "You saying you wouldn't have tried to kill him if it came from me instead?"

"I didn't try to kill him," he mutters, almost pouting. "I just wanted to scare him a bit."

"Well, you did that. I haven't seen or heard from him since. I think he transferred to another college."

"I know he did."

"Huh?" I ask, looking down into his eyes, frowning when I see the amusement there.

"You really think I would have been able to sleep at night in there if I knew he was still around? I made Phoenix and Tryst go and threaten him before he left the hospital."

"When did you do that?"

"As soon as they let me call them," he answers, his cold fingers brushing the backs of my knees. "My first call was you. And my second. And my third. But you never picked up," he reminds me, sinking back into my body with a heavy exhale. "I used my fourth call to make sure that little fucker never laid eyes on you again."

I try to stay pissed at him and the boys for doing that —I'm *really* trying—but I'm still hung up on the other things he said.

My first call was you.

"Are you mad at me, Atty?"

"Yes."

"You wanna hurt me?"

"Yes," he says honestly, reaching up to cup the back of my neck. "But you already know I won't. I *can't*. No matter what happens. I'll kill myself before I ever hurt you for real."

I nod and chew the inside of my cheek, reaching over him to grab the tequila from the bottom step.

"Truth or dare?" he asks.

"Truth," I blurt out, surprising us both.

He grins like he's won this little game of his. I expect him to be an asshole about it, but it seems he's not shameless enough to force me to admit things I'm not sure I'll ever say out loud again.

"Why aren't you wearing any panties right now?"

I raise a brow at that. "You know why."

"Say it anyway."

"Because," I start, dipping my head to press my lips to his ear. "I like the way these fishnets feel against my clit every time I move."

He curses and turns around to face me, forcing himself between my legs until he's right on top of me, the steps digging painfully into my back. "Your turn," he says.

"Truth or dare?"

"Dare."

Oh fuck.

My brows pull in, and I open my mouth, but instead of saying what I'm supposed to say, I say the complete opposite. "I dare you to drop the act."

"What?"

"I know you're holding back," I rasp, even though my head is screaming at me to shut the fuck up. "Stop pretending to be something you're not and show me the boy I fell for."

The look on his face is pure evil, but I'm not afraid of him. I'm all keyed up now, squirming beneath him, impatiently waiting to see what he'll do next.

After what feels like minutes but is probably only a few seconds, he curls his fingers over the tank top I'm wearing and rips it down the middle, just like I thought about him doing when I put it on tonight. I'm not wearing a bra, so my chest is fully exposed to him. He clamps his teeth around my nipple, and a squeal escapes me at the sting, but he doesn't let up. He bites me harder, punishing me for what I did to him, laughing when I whimper and try to pull him off by his hair.

"Atty, stop."

He does stop, but only to lift his head and move on to the other nipple, giving it the same painful treatment as he did the first one. I'm damn near screaming now, digging my nails into his scalp and bucking my hips up, desperate to throw him off me. It fucking *hurts*, but this is what I asked for, isn't it? To face the *real* Atticus head-on. *My* Atticus. The one who does and takes what he wants, whenever he wants…fuck the consequences.

"It's my turn again," he says, easing up a little to suck away the sting. "Truth or dare?"

"Dare," I choke out, like we both knew I would.

"I dare you to tell me to stop like you mean it," he says against my skin. "Tell me no, baby."

"No."

"*Like you mean it*, Vi."

"No," I say again, louder this time. "Get off me."

He sighs like he's disappointed and sucks on the underside of my breast, marking my flesh as I fight and struggle beneath him. But he's so much stronger than me, and I can't get out from under his grip. He laughs some more and then moves his mouth up to my neck, pinning my hands down on either side of me as he gives me a hickey there too.

"Fucking beautiful," he whispers, tilting his head to do the same thing on the other side. "I love it when you walk around with my marks on you."

"You're insane," I grit out, snatching one of my hands away to hit him in the face.

He pinches his eyes shut at the sudden pain, and I take the opportunity to reach for the almost full bottle lying on the step by my feet, picking it up and swinging it into the side of his head. The glass doesn't smash—I didn't hit him that hard—but it's enough for me to gain the upper hand, to scramble out from beneath him and make a run for it.

"*I'm* insane?" he calls after me, breathing out a laugh as he stands up. "Nasty little bitch."

"Fuck you!"

"You better run fast!" he shouts. "Because when I catch you, that's *exactly* what's happening."

CHAPTER 5
ATTICUS

I shake my head with a huff and pick up the bottle she clocked me with, watching her back for the third time tonight while I take a drink.

That's my fucking girl.

I smile to myself and start to go after her, but just as my feet hit the bottom step, I hear what sounds like a cut off scream coming from inside the cabin.

"A—"

"Shut up," someone else hisses, and my smile turns into a full-on grin, because I'd know that voice anywhere.

The door opens before I can open it myself, and Phoenix steps out, pulling the door shut behind him and blocking it with his body.

"Were you watching us just now?" I ask him, eyeing

him in his black hoodie with the hood pulled up over his blond head of hair.

"No."

"Don't lie to me, Phoenix," I singsong, slowly stepping closer as I swing the bottle at my side, ready to clock *him* with it if I need to.

"Look, it's dark, okay? I didn't see shit. Chill the fuck out and go play with your girl."

I narrow my eyes at that, suspicious. Since when does he encourage me to *play* with Violet? Any other night he'd be bitching and trying to convince me to leave her be.

"Why? So you can stay here and play with yours?"

"She's not mine."

"You want her to be?" I ask, raising a brow when he says nothing. "Let me see her."

"No." He shakes his head and sidesteps to stop me from passing him, eyes wide as if he's nervous. "Not this one."

I stare at his white painted face for a minute, trying to figure out what's got him acting so weird all of a sudden. But then I realize I don't really give a fuck what he's got going on in there. Violet's out here somewhere without a fucking shirt on, and that's always gonna be more important to me.

"All right," I say, grinning again as I back away. "Have fun with her, brother."

NIGHTMARE

"You know I can hear you, right?" I call into the darkness, turning around when I hear something hit the ground behind me. "You still suck at this game, baby."

The big rock she just threw rolls left to a stop, so I move right, knowing it came from that way. She lets out a whispered curse and starts running again. My heart races as I chase her through the woods, the leaves and gravel crunching loudly beneath our boots, so much adrenaline filling my bloodstream that I feel like I could stay high off it for weeks.

I'm right on her tail within seconds, making her scream when I catch her wrist and yank her back to me, her body slamming into mine. Her lungs empty out, but I don't give her a chance to recover, picking her up and throwing her over my shoulder, narrowly avoiding another hit to the balls when she kicks her feet.

"Stop fighting me."

"Put me *down*," she growls. "You know I hate being carried like a child."

I do know that. But if she wants to keep acting like one and having these little temper tantrums of hers, then I'll keep treating her like one.

I walk her a few more feet until she gives up and relaxes in my arms, then I look around to make sure there are no stragglers over here. Once I'm sure no one's gonna see my girlfriend's tits, I stop right where I am and put her down on her feet, keeping hold of her hand just in case she decides to bolt again the first chance she gets.

"It's my turn," I say to her, lifting my thumb to smudge the dirt on her cheek.

"No," she breathes out. "I'm really done this time, Atty. You win."

But I don't win until she's mine again.

Those are the rules, and she knows it.

"Truth or dare, Vi?"

She looks exhausted, but my brave girl still looks me dead in the eye and says, "Dare."

I hold her gaze while I take the crumpled, folded sheets of paper from my back pocket, watching her face as she looks down at my hand. She reacts exactly the way I knew she would. First, there's confusion, then realization, surprise, and then finally…rage.

"Where did you get those?!" she shouts, snatching the letters I wrote her from prison and clutching them to her bare chest.

"I found them in your pillow."

"You went to my apartment?"

"It's *my* apartment too."

"Not anymore." She lifts her chin at me in defiance, and I give her a tight-lipped smile, barely containing my own anger as I crowd her space and wrap my hand around her neck.

"You're pushing me, baby."

Her jaw tightens, but she doesn't fight me. I squeeze

her flesh a little harder, but I don't cut her air off completely. Just enough to put her on edge a bit.

"You have my lighter."

It's not a question, but she still answers, "Yeah, so?"

"Take it out."

Still holding my letters to her chest, using them to cover herself, she lifts her foot up and reaches down inside her boot, struggling to pull it out with her throat in my hand. Once she's got it, she drops her leg and holds the lighter up for me, but I don't take it.

"I dare you to burn them."

"What?"

"You heard me."

Her eyes are wide now, her panic overtaking the anger. She does nothing for what feels like a really long time.

I don't remember every word I wrote to her in that cell. I was out of my mind when I wrote those things—real nasty things. But something tells me she could recite them in her sleep.

"How many times have you read them?"

"Hundreds," she admits, swallowing against my palm. "They're mine, Atty."

"I don't care. Burn them."

"*No.*"

We stare each other out a moment, and then I take the lighter from her, using my free hand to flip the black top over and strike the flame. I hold it up between us, using the light to look into her pretty eyes, moving her head around to study every inch of her perfect little face. She still looks mad at me, but she also looks terrified I might actually do this. Fear isn't something I usually see on her. Not when she's looking at me.

"I fucking love you, Violet Sinclair," I whisper, remembering that part. "That's what I wrote at the end of each one, right? That's what you're holding on to."

She doesn't say anything at first, the papers crumpling even more inside her tightening fist. "You told me you hated me."

"I didn't mean it."

"Maybe, but still…"

"Damn it, Violet, do you know how hard it was in there without you?" I hiss, and her gaze drops to my hand on my dick. "Not just this, but *all* of it. You fucking *left* me."

"You left me first."

I pull back at that, using my grip on her neck to get her to look at me again. "Is *that* what this was about? You wanted to punish me for getting myself thrown in jail?"

"No," she defends, but then her voice gets smaller. "Not really. I don't know."

"What *do* you know, Vi?" I bite out, my patience wearing thin.

"I know you're fucking crazy. I know your obsession

with me is toxic as fuck and I needed to get out. I know you're bad for me and I'm better off without you."

"That's your mother putting words in your mouth. They're not yours."

She shrugs, not denying it. "Maybe she's right."

"*Maybe* she's a cunt."

"Atty."

"I'm sorry."

She sighs heavily, but then a teeny little smile creeps across her lips, and I swear to God, it feels like my heart runs and smashes itself against the inside of my chest, desperate to get to her, begging for a taste of what's mine.

Not caring if it earns me another slap to the face, I take my shot and drop both hands to her waist, roughly pressing my lips to hers without warning. She doesn't hit me, but she does freeze up a bit. And then she whispers a curse and kisses me back.

She's fucking kissing me back.

Her fingers move through my hair as she gives me her tongue to suck on, and the relief rushing through me almost knocks me on my ass. Unable to stand up anymore, I fall to my knees in front of her and look up at her face, running my palms over her fishnets. She licks my taste off her lips, and I yank her to the ground with me, forcing her down on her back and pulling her toward me by the backs of her knees. She winces at the scrape of the branches on her bare flesh, and I reach under her to grab the bottle I must have dropped before, wedged beneath her hip. I toss it over my shoulder and lean in to kiss her again, making it messy as fuck and dirtying her up as much as I can. With that goal in mind, I run my tongue over her mouth and cheek, then down to her neck, grinning when I see the forgotten lighter next to her head and the pile of dirty letters she's lying on.

"I win."

CHAPTER 6
VIOLET

I can't let him win.

He's *bad for me*, goddamn it, and I can't let him slip his way back inside my head and fuck me up all over again.

I *can't...*

But I'm not burning those letters, and I'm sure as shit not stopping him from sliding his tongue all over me. He's at my collarbone now, licking a path over the marks he put on me outside the cabin before. The mix of the chill in the air combined with the heat of his mouth is making me shiver, but I'm not cold. I'm burning all over, my legs falling open as if they have a mind of their own, inviting him to lie on top of me and wedge himself between them. He does just that, his hand moving down beneath my skirt to rub my clit. I arch my back up into him, needing more, impatiently pushing his head down to get him to move faster.

"You want something?" he asks with a smile in his voice, taunting me.

"You know what I want," I force out between my teeth.

Before I can even blink, he sits back on his heels and rips my fishnets open, baring my pussy to him. "Is that it?" he rasps, and I shake my head.

"More."

He smirks and looks down between my legs, gathering the wetness there before he slips his finger inside me. Not all the way, though; just enough to make my walls clench around him.

"You wouldn't let anyone else in here, would you, baby?"

"No," I say, partly because it's the truth, but I'm mostly saying it just to please him.

He loves asking me shit like that and hearing my answers.

"That's my good girl," he says softly, pushing his digit deeper until I can feel the black, chunky ring on his middle finger nudging at my entrance.

I squirm and shift my hips, my mixed feelings about that damn ring rushing up to the surface. Of course he notices, his smirk turning vicious as he watches my face.

This motherfucker.

Last time he did this—the day I bought him the

stupid ring for his birthday last year—I was scared shitless it was gonna get lost up there. It didn't, but still. I don't know if I want him to do it again, but I don't open my mouth in time to say no. Not that he'd stop if I told him to, anyway. No never *really* means no with me and Atticus. We've known each other for so long that we can always tell what the other is thinking. He knows my limits just as I know his—not that he has many—and he'll only stop if he thinks I really want him to.

Eyes on mine, he moves the ring up and places it on the tip of his finger, turning it the other way around so it's face up when he turns his palm upside down. Then he carefully eases that finger inside me and fucks me with it, hooking it upward, the square part of the ring rubbing the spot inside me that makes me moan every time he touches it.

"Atty," I say, confused, because I'm freaking out but feeling good all at once. "Fuck."

"What is it, baby? You need my tongue to make it better?"

I nod helplessly, and he gets to work, holding himself up on one hand as he lowers his face between my legs. He doesn't tease me. His tongue lashes at my clit, and he brings my hand up to the back of his head, encouraging me to fuck his mouth with my pussy.

"Harder," he demands, so I pull his hair until I know it hurts, eagerly rolling my hips up to match the pace of his finger. "There you go, dirty girl."

God fucking help me with this guy.

Licking my clit just the way I like it, he eats me out for so long that his jaw must be killing him, but he doesn't stop. Not until he knows he's got me dancing on the edge.

"Asshole," I growl, kicking at him when he sits up and pulls his finger out.

"You wanna come?" he asks, snatching my ankle to keep my foot still. "Take it."

I narrow my eyes and place the sole of my other boot on his chest, pushing him down until he's the one lying on his back in the dirt.

He might let me fuck him, but I already know *he* won't fuck *me*. Not yet. He told me so in letter number thirteen, that he'd drag this out for as long as it takes and make me beg for it.

I may have secretly been hoping he'd cave when it finally came to it, but he's a stubborn prick and it's always push and pull with him. He's unpredictable. I can read his emotions like a book in the moment, but at the same time, I never know what's coming next with Atticus, and that's what I love so much about him. He's exciting and fun and so different than any other person I've ever met.

And he's *mine*.

Whether I want him or not, I've got him for life.

Forcing myself to stop thinking so much, I crawl over him on my hands and knees and swing my leg over his body, sitting on his legs to undo the button on his jeans. He doesn't help me take his cock out or even bother to lift his ass. He just holds on to my thighs and sucks on his bottom lip, devouring my body with his eyes. I'm pretty sure I'm covered in dirt, but he doesn't seem to mind. He likes me like this—filthy—especially when he's the cause, and I know he's thinking about all the other places he could leave his mark on me tonight, whether it be with his teeth or his hands. The thought makes me shiver.

"Are you cold?" he asks, knowing that's not the reason.

"Shut up."

He grins like a madman, groaning when I pull his dick out of his pants and dip my head to spit on it. "*Fuck*, baby. Do that again."

I do, stroking it in my fist a few times to cover it with my saliva. He clenches his jaw and digs his fingertips into my flesh, like it's killing him to lie there and do nothing. I know this is meant to be a punishment for me, but he's making me feel like a fucking queen.

Leaving my clothes exactly as they are, I lift my skirt and move forward on my knees, lowering myself down to rub my pussy on his cock. I haven't had him inside me for over half a year, and even though I'm sure it won't hurt as much as it did the first time, I still sink down on him slowly, just the tip at first to test the waters.

"Don't be a cock tease, Vi," he warns. "I'll hurt you."

"But I like it when you make it hurt," I say sweetly, throwing his own words back at him from earlier.

He moves like he's about to grab me, so I wrap my hand around his throat like he's done to me so many times, shoving his head down against the ground. He grunts, and I grind down on him the rest of the way, until there's not an inch of space left between us.

"*God...*" he whispers, more to himself than me. "Move."

Knowing that part *is* for me, I give us what we both want and move my hips on him, pushing my ass out to rub my clit on his pelvis. I've always loved this position, but I really don't have the thighs for it, and the way he's looking at me right now is distracting as fuck.

"I love it when you ride me like this," he moans, squeezing my hip and guiding me back and forth. "You're so pretty, baby."

Fuck my heart, the praise-loving little whore.

"Will you stop talking?"

He lets out a quiet laugh, leaning up on one elbow to grab my ass with his free hand. "You sure you don't wanna hear it?"

"I'm sure."

"You don't wanna hear how hot I think it is when you use me? When you grind this wet little pussy on my cock like it's your own personal fuck toy?"

"No."

"What if I tell you how many times I moaned your

name into my pillow when I was in prison?" He keeps going, turning my face to put his mouth next to my ear. "On one of the nights you hung up on my call, I fucked my own hand and pretended it was your throat. I thought about stuffing you with my dick until you couldn't breathe. Right here," he adds, tapping his finger against the base of my neck. "I came so fucking hard, Vi. It was everywhere."

I whimper and rock myself on him faster, using my fingers to play with my clit, desperate to find release. But he's still not moving, and I can't get the angle right.

"Come on, baby," he urges. "You can do it."

"I can't," I whine, dropping my face to his neck. "Atty, fuck me back."

"Not until you beg me for it."

"Please," I say without argument. "I'm sorry I left you in there. Please, Atty."

"Tell me you still love me."

I growl and bash my fist into his chest. "That's not part of the fucking game."

"My game," he taunts, nipping at my cheek. "My rules."

I heave out an aggravated breath and push him back down, looking right at him and digging my sharp nails into his flesh. "I still love you, okay? It doesn't matter wh—"

Before I can finish, he grabs the back of my head with one hand and my ass with the other, pulling me down and holding me tight against him as he fucks up into me. *Hard.* I cry out and put my arms on the ground either side of his head, trying to hold myself steady, my thighs tightening as I feel myself coming all over his cock.

"Keep going," he orders halfway through my orgasm. "It doesn't matter…"

"What I do," I add, moaning into his neck. "I can't stop myself."

"I know, baby," he says softly, tangling my hair with his fingers as he waits for me to ride it out. "I can't either."

"Do you want to?"

"Never."

CHAPTER 7
ATTICUS

As soon as she's finished coming, she drops all her weight on my chest, exhausted. I smile up at the sky and gently roll her onto her back, placing my t-shirt out beneath her to stop the ground from scratching her up more than it already has. Knowing her thighs are probably aching from riding my dick for all of five minutes, I stretch her legs out and rub them better for her, massaging the feeling back into them.

"What are you doing?" she asks, cracking an eye open to watch me.

"Making you feel good before I fuck you up all over again."

She chuckles and tilts her head to look down at my dick. It's still rock hard, leaking pre-cum at the sight of her, like it knows who it belongs to and it wants back in. I wrap my fingers around it and take in her pussy, but just as I'm about to move back between her legs, she stops me with a lazy shake of her head.

"Not yet," she says. "Show me."

I raise a brow at her, because the spoiled little brat is in no position to be making all these demands. "What?"

"Show me how you made yourself come thinking about me. I wanna see."

"You think I care what you want?"

"You care." She leans up and crosses her long legs at the ankle, biting the tip of her finger in a way that makes her look more devil than angel. "And you and I both know you could never say no to me. I say jump and you s—"

"Lie the fuck down."

She smirks and does as she's told, following my every move as she waits for me to come to her. I climb on top of her on all fours and tap her wet pussy with my cock, stroking it once from the base to the tip. Closing my eyes, I imagine I'm facedown on the bed I woke up on not twelve hours ago. I push my face into my forearm next to her head and use her body like I used that shitty mattress, rutting into her as I fuck my own fist.

She lies still, and I think about fucking her throat again. The night I was so fucking angry with her I could barely see straight. I was a nasty fucker to her inside my head, tying her down on our bed and straddling her face, watching the tears leaking out of her eyes, making her gag and retch on my dick. And once I knew she couldn't take it anymore, I pushed four fingers inside her mouth along with my cock and made her choke on those too.

"*Violet*," I growl into my arm, biting it to keep quiet. "I need you."

She takes my jaw in her hand, and I can feel her eyes on the side of my face, her thumb stroking back and forth as she watches me. Unable to stop myself, I pull her head back by her hair and kiss her, sealing her mouth with mine and feeding her my tongue. She moans, and I rock my hips harder. My chest brushes her stiff nipples with every slide, and I can feel how wet her pussy is on the back of my knuckles, coating my hand with her juices.

"Spread your lips for me, baby. I wanna come on your clit."

Breathing hot and hard against my mouth, she lets go of my face and reaches down between us to do as she's told. I pull back and look down to watch what she's doing, groaning at the feel of my dick pulsing in my hand, the pleasure racing up my spine.

"Lift your ass up," I demand. "Hold it open just like that."

She does, and my entire body shudders as I point my dick down and spill my release all over her pussy, careful not to waste a drop. Head still spinning, I kneel between her legs and hold her ass for her, spreading my cum around to make sure she's covered in it. Then I scoop it all up with two fingers and shove it deep inside her.

She gasps. "Atty—"

"Are you still on the pill?"

Please say no.

She pales, and like the sick fuck I am, I'm suddenly way more excited than I should be. It's such a stupid thing to wish for, because I'm nowhere near ready to be a dad, but if I could put a baby in her—*my* baby—she'd have no choice but t—

"I'll get the morning-after pill tomorrow."

"Okay," I say, secretly hoping I can distract her enough to forget.

"What about…"

'What?" I ask, amused when I realize what's going through her head. "You think I fucked my cell mate and caught something in there?"

"You could have."

She's right. I could have. But I didn't and she knows it.

"I would never cheat on you, Vi. That's not me."

She nods, chewing the inside of her cheek. "I know."

"So what's the problem?" I ask, averting my eyes back to my fingers in her pussy, still slowly fucking my cum into her.

Her eyes narrow into thin slits, and I smirk right at her, laughing when she sits up and tries to smack me upside the head. "You twisted motherf—"

Just as she lands in my lap, I put my hand over her mouth and lift a finger to my lips to shush her, my ears perking at the sound of branches snapping in the distance. Violet's head turns as she listens too—the low voices getting closer. Knowing there are guys around here somewhere, I quickly grab my t-shirt and throw it on over her head, covering her half naked body with it. We stand up, and I leave my dick hanging out of my pants, checking her to make sure the hem comes down beneath her ass, considering that slutty little skirt she's wearing does nothing to hide it. Satisfied no one will see anything, I tuck myself back in and zip my pants, watching as she crouches down to pick all the letters up off the ground. She picks up her own shirt next—which is useless and torn to shit—shaking it off before she moves to clean herself with it. I snatch it from her and throw it up into a tree, pulling her in and locking my arms around her waist.

"*Hey.*"

"Leave it." I squeeze her ass, my dick hardening again when I feel how soaked she is down there. "I like knowing you're walking around with my cum dripping out between your legs."

Her eyes darken, and she wraps her hand around the back of my neck, pushing up on her tiptoes to speak in my ear. "You're sick, Atty."

"Mhmm," I say, sneaking my tongue out to lick her cheek. "Does it make your pussy hurt?"

She breathes out a chuckle and shakes her head at me, taking my hand before she bends over to grab the bottle of tequila. "I need another drink."

CHAPTER 8
VIOLET

"What was it like in there?"

"Prison?" he asks, shrugging when I nod. "It sucked, Vi."

I pinch my lips to the side and avert my eyes. I'm leaning back between his legs with my letters in my lap, putting them back in the order they came in. He's got one arm around my middle with his chin resting on my shoulder, holding his lighter up for me so I can see what I'm doing.

"Because of me?"

"A little bit, yeah," he says, and it punches me right in the gut. "I mean, it would have been a hell of a lot easier if I hadn't lost my mind worrying about you and if you'd been around for me to talk to. But prison's still prison. It would have sucked either way."

I think about that a moment while I run my thumb

over the scratchy ink on the pages, catching a few glimpses of his words as I go.

You're gonna pay for this, you little bitch.

You can't hide from me forever.

Baby, you're killing me.

I'm coming for you.

"Do you feel guilty?" he asks, probably seeing the same things I'm seeing.

"Sometimes," I admit. "Do you? For what you did to Jared?"

"No," he says honestly, because of course he doesn't. "I told him to stay the fuck away and he didn't listen. He deserved what he got."

"Atty, you almost killed him."

"And I would have done it for real if you hadn't stopped him from kissing you."

"You know about that?"

"Baby, I know everything when it comes to you," he teases, pressing his face to mine to kiss my cheek, watching me read a minute before he speaks again. "Are we really not gonna talk about it?"

"Talk about what?" I feign indifference, my heart racing with nerves.

"Someone paid for my lawyers, Vi," he says slowly, turning my chin when I refuse to look at him. "They paid off the judge too. I know it was you."

"I—"

"Don't lie to me."

Fuck.

"I didn't get you out," I whisper. "I just got you a little less time."

"Five to ten years less is a lot more than a little."

"Yeah, well…" I clear my throat, pulling my face out of his grip. "You might be fucking crazy, but I wasn't gonna leave you in there for *years*."

He chuckles and drops his chin back on my shoulder. "Thank you," he says, and I say nothing. "Did you use all the money your grandmother left you?"

"Only most of it. I've got enough left to finish college and pay the bills."

"What about the creepy house you wanted at the top of the hill?"

"I'll get there," I say quietly. "Eventually."

He goes quiet then, and I swallow the anxiety creeping up my throat as our thoughts align as one. I said *I'll* get there, not *we,* like it used to be.

"What about you?" I ask in a lame-ass attempt to change the subject. "Are you coming back to college now you're out?"

"I burned down one of their dorm rooms," he reminds me. "I think I'm expelled."

A laugh bubbles out of me, and I nod. "Yeah. Probably."

"God, I missed your laugh." He sighs, tightening his arm around my waist so hard he's damn near crushing my rib cage. "Baby, look at me."

"I don't want to."

I hear the clicking sound of his lighter closing right before we're suddenly clouded in darkness. "Is that better?"

I nod, and he rakes his fingers through my hair, tipping my head back to get me to face him. I can't see his eyes now—mine haven't had time to adjust back to the dark—but I know they're locked in on me, like he's trying to slink his way into my skull and organize the mess in there. To get me to feel the things I'm desperately trying not to feel.

Instead of speaking, he kisses my bottom lip, then the top one, coaxing my mouth open with his tongue. His hand comes around to the side of my neck, and he uses his thumb to tilt my face, controlling the kiss. It's not messy or rough this time. He's kissing me like we've got all the time in the world. Like we'll get a million more of these before we die.

"Baby," he breathes into my mouth. "I wanna come home."

"Atty."

"Please," he begs, stunning me, because I don't think I've *ever* heard him say that word before.

Shaking myself out of his trance, I try to stand my ground. "Not yet. I can't be with you again until you prove to me it'll be different this time. I'm not gonna repeat the last six years for the rest of my life, Atty. It's not happening."

I still can't see him properly, but I can feel the moment this rare sweet side of him crumples to dust. In the next second, I'm landing flat on my back and he's hovering over me, his breath against my cheek as his hand comes back to my throat.

There he is.

"I'm only gonna say this once, so listen properly," he growls against my flesh. "I'm not leaving these woods without you by my side. So you might as well stop fucking around with me and skip to the part where I get to take my girl home."

"No." I shove his hand away from my neck, fighting him when he tries to throttle me again. "You can't just force your way back into my life and expect me to lie down and take it."

"That's *exactly* what you're gonna do." He chuckles like the evil bastard he is, effortlessly pinning my swinging arms to the dirt above my head. "You think you can get rid of me?" he taunts. "I'll haunt you, Vi. I'll make your life a living hell."

"You already do that," I retort, lifting my head until I'm right up in his face, my nose touching his. "What have I got to lose?"

"*This*," he says simply, straightening up fast to pull my skirt down to my ankles. "Me and you. The way it's supposed to be."

He balls it up and tosses it to the side, then he hooks his fingers into the hole he made in my fishnets and rips them open even more. They were ruined anyway, but now they're nothing but scraps; the flimsy material hanging loosely around my knees. He leaves my boots on and pushes his t-shirt up to my collarbone, grabbing the backs of my knees to spread my legs out as far as they'll go. I'm already dripping with his cum, so it takes no effort at all for him to shove his cock deep inside me. And he wastes no time. He starts fucking me relentlessly, like he's *trying* to hurt me, his hip bones smashing against my ass with every hard hit.

"*Fuck*," I cry out, squeezing my eyes shut at the pain. "Atty, that's too much."

"You can take it," he assures me. "Relax your hips and stop trying to push me out."

I take a breath and do as he says, relieved to find he's right. It doesn't hurt as much when I stop fighting it, but I can't help the way my body keeps trying to reject him, the way my legs keep closing to try to relieve some of the pressure. His nostrils flare and he grabs my thighs again, leaning on them with his hands so I have no choice but to keep them open.

I'm whining and writhing beneath him, licking my fingers to get them ready for my clit. He spits on my pelvis, and I eagerly scoop it up, using his saliva to play with myself. Feeling braver now, I arch my back up for him and watch him fuck me, pinching my own nipple as I run my eyes over the muscles carved into his flesh. After just a couple more minutes, his dick starts to feel good, and then *really* fucking good, stretching and filling me to my limit.

"That's it, baby girl," he rasps with a grin. "Damn. Look at you."

I grin back at his praise and squeeze my nipple a little harder, pulling my brows in when he reaches over to grab the tequila. Before I can protest, he uncaps it and pours the freezing cold liquid over my neck, breasts, and stomach, biting his own lip as he soaks me with it.

"*Fucker*!" I squeal. "What the hell are you doing?!"

"I want you sticky," he says, bending over to lick some off my chest.

I huff out my annoyance and pull his hot body down over mine, using him to keep me warm. "You're a nightmare."

"I'm *your* nightmare."

Yeah. He's right about that.

"Kiss me," I say, and he smashes his lips against mine.

He devours me. Consumes me.

I run my nails over his scalp, feeling his soft hair between my fingers. He hums and gives me his tongue, licking into my mouth, curling it in and out to match the steady new pace he's got going on my pussy. I pull back for air and turn his face to get to his neck, kissing him there for a bit. Just as I'm about to give him a hickey of his own, something catches my eye and I do a double take, squinting into the darkness at the couple tearing each other's clothes off just a few feet away from us.

"Atty, is that…?" I trail off, my eyes widening when I realize who the girl is. "Holy shit."

"What?"

"Tryst and Andie," I whisper, tipping my chin in their direction. "Look."

He tenses and turns his head toward them, pulling his t-shirt down over my breasts, slowly, like he doesn't want them to catch any sudden movements and look over here.

I stare in slack-jawed wonder as Trystan kisses the shit out of my best friend, squeezing her ass and wrapping her legs around his waist. She has a boyfriend, but that's not even the part that's so shocking to me. Andie hates Trystan. *Really* hates him.

Or at least I thought she did.

"What are they doing?" Atticus asks, sounding just as confused as I am.

I close my mouth and then open it again, completely at a loss for words.

"Maybe we should go somewhere else," I suggest after another minute, but neither of us makes any move to leave.

Our eyes stay hooked on the other couple as Trystan spins Andie around and kisses her neck from behind, pulling on her tight blonde curls to give himself a better angle.

Atticus moves once inside me, slow and long, and a sound slips out before I can stop it.

Fuck.

His hand blocks my moans from spilling out, and he lowers himself down to cover me. "No moaning," he warns in my ear. "If you let him hear you, I'll stop."

Not *them*. *Him*.

Andie whimpers then, and my pussy clenches around Atticus's dick, my cheeks heating when I realize they're both staring right at us. They're on their knees now, him saying something in her ear from behind and squeezing her breasts through her dress.

"You wanna watch?" Atticus asks me, tilting his head at Andie. "I think she likes it."

I can't speak with his hand pressed tightly against my mouth, but yeah, I think so too. I can see how hot she is for this, her chest heaving with harsh breaths.

Taking my silence as a yes, he looks over at Trystan and glares. "Eyes off."

Trystan chuckles darkly and goes back to kissing Andie's neck, pulling her dress up over her ass while he uses his other hand to work on his jeans. I can tell the moment he enters her, because she cries out and tips her head back on his shoulder, lifting her arm to hold on to the back of his neck.

Damn, they look hot together.

I never would have pictured it before now, but now that I'm seeing it, I can't look away.

Atticus's fingertips are probably bruising my cheek as he grinds his cock into my pussy, all the while keeping his gaze locked on me. I can barely breathe, pulling just enough oxygen in through my nostrils to keep me conscious. It's making me dizzy, but I love it. I love how rough and cruel he is. How possessive he is over me. *My Atticus.*

The way it's supposed to be.

Just then, Andie screams, and I turn my head that way again, seeing Trystan pinching her bare nipple and playing with her clit as he fucks into her from behind. I curse and grab Atticus's ass, rubbing myself on him, wanting to come at the same time she does.

"Filthy little girl," he teases. "You like watching your best friends fuck?"

I mumble a yes beneath his palm, and he pushes down on my mouth harder in warning. I run my hands up his back and drag my nails down as payback, slow but deep. It makes him groan and fuck me harder, just like I wanted.

Andie sounds like she's coming, and Atticus makes sure I'm right there with her, my arms and legs tightening around his body as I shiver and shake beneath him.

"Fuck yes. Squeeze it out of me, baby," he rasps quietly, just for me. "I'm gonna fill you up with so much cum. All night. I'm gonna fuck you every time my dick gets hard again."

Unable to respond to that, I just lie here and jerk at

the aftershocks. Our bodies are pressed tightly together as he spills his release into my pussy. Once he's done, he finally lets go of my mouth and pulls out to lie on his left side, blocking me from Trystan's view. I feel Atticus moving, but I'm not sure what he's doing. I'm suddenly too tired to care. But then I feel something cold and hard pushing into my pussy, and I'm back on high alert.

"What is that?"

"Shh," he whispers. "Stop talking and show me your hole."

Jesus Christ.

He's got a fucking butt plug—probably the one from my dresser—the sneaky prick.

He gives me an amused look that says *I'm waiting*, and I take a deep breath, reaching down beneath my legs to spread my ass cheeks for him.

"Wider."

I feel the cold air hitting my asshole, and it makes me shiver in anticipation. He slides the silver plug in and out of my pussy a few more times, coating it with his cum. Then he moves it down to my ass, twisting it around to prepare me. Once I'm ready, he gently pushes it inside, and I gasp, squirming a little at the feeling. It's been so long since I had anything in there. I got myself off more times than I can count when he was in prison, but never with anything more than my fingers in my pussy. Not because I didn't *want* to fuck myself with my vibrator, but because he has this weird love-hate relationship with it and the rest of my toys. *He* loves using them on me, but I know he wouldn't like it if I used them on myself without him there. I shouldn't have cared, but I'm stupid and I did.

I've always been stupid for him.

His eyes lock in on mine like he knows exactly what I'm thinking about, and then he's over me again, roughly shoving two fingers inside me. "If I find out you've had a dick in here that isn't mine…" he warns, pushing down on my walls and nudging the plug. "I don't give a shit if it was plastic. I'll rip this little pussy apart and make you bleed."

I grin up at him, laughing when it just makes him madder. "I guess you'll never know."

He growls and kisses me, sucking on my bottom lip so hard I'm sure he's leaving a mark, his teeth denting my skin.

I hear someone cough, so I pull away from Atticus and peek over his shoulder, only just remembering we're not alone. Trystan is kneeling beside Andie, shaking his head at us with a smile as he buttons his jeans. Andie's sitting on the ground with her knees pulled up to her chest, scrunching her nose at us in confusion.

"You two are fucking weird," she says, making me and Trystan laugh.

Atticus passes me my skirt, and I slide it back on, removing my boots to pull the ruined fishnets from around my ankles. Once I've got my shoes back on, he takes my hand and helps me to my feet, tightening his grip when I move toward Andie. I glance at him over my shoulder, and he frowns, looking down at the empty bottle of tequila he's holding.

"Five minutes," he says, although I can tell he's furious about it.

"Twenty."

"Ten," he bites out, and I roll my lips with a nod.

"Meet us at the bar," Trystan says to Andie, blowing her a kiss when she just glares up at him.

He tips his chin at Atticus, and the two boys walk off toward the main party, disappearing into the darkness between the trees. I sit down next to Andie and rest my head on her shoulder, wrapping my hands around her arm and hugging it to my chest.

I haven't even said anything yet, but I know she notices the shift in me already.

I may not have admitted it—to her or myself—but I was miserable and heartbroken when we started this night together, and now I can't stop fucking smiling for some reason. It probably looks creepy, so I force myself to stop and relax my face.

She opens her mouth to say something to me, but I cut her off before she can get a word in. "Don't even think about it. You first."

She sighs and bites her lip. "Don't judge me."

I raise a brow and make a point to look down at my body—at the bite marks and the bruises and the dirt all over me, the scent of tequila soaking the men's shirt I'm wearing, the cum between my legs and the plug in my asshole, all at the hands of my walking red flag of an ex-boyfriend.

"I won't."

CHAPTER 9
ATTICUS

"You got her back."

"Almost," I say to Trystan, scanning the bottles of alcohol me and the boys stashed behind this tree earlier, about a minute walk away from the fire we lit. "I'm working on it."

I find some of Violet's favorite tequila, and then the two of us continue walking toward the bar, grabbing two solo cups to pour ourselves a drink each. It's lighter and louder over here. The music's still blaring, the partygoers acting a lot more crazy and drunk than they were when I was here earlier. There are couples and threesomes everywhere, grinding and dry-fucking each other, and there's even a guy on his knees throating another guy's dick in the middle of it all, earning a few heated glances from the people around them.

"Why didn't you tell us you were getting out today?" Tryst shouts so I can hear him over the chaos.

"Because you're all big mouths," I shout back.

The random guy I gave my drugs to earlier walks by us, and I stop him to take a pink pill out of the bag he's holding, popping it onto my tongue with a smile. Trystan snorts as he takes a pill for himself, but he doesn't say anything else, which is weird because he usually doesn't shut up. I pull my brows in and study his face a moment, wondering why he's being so quiet. Tonight's not the first time I've seen his dick, so I know it's not about me or what we just did, but it *is* the first time I've seen him put it in the girl who's despised him for as long as I've known her. He teased the shit out of her back in high school, and even though it wasn't that bad—I wouldn't call him a bully or anything—she's a snippy little thing and she can't take a joke. Not when it comes to him.

"What's up with you and Andie?"

He smirks to himself but doesn't answer, giving me no clues as to what he's thinking. I can usually read my friends better than this, considering we've known each other our whole lives, but tonight I've got nothing—not with him or with Phoenix.

I'm the crazy one out of the three of us, the one outsiders tend to stay away from. Phoenix is the nice one, the sensible boy we can all rely on when it counts. And Trystan's a bit of a wild card. He's got a heart of gold and this annoying, happy attitude, but he also has a mean side, and he can be a nasty motherfucker if you give him a reason.

He sips his drink, his eyes tracking something over the rim of his cup, and I turn my head to follow his line of sight. The girls are back, hands linked together, as usual, laughing with each other as they walk toward us. Violet doesn't give a shit about the side-eyes she's getting, completely at ease and unashamed of the state I left her in.

Jesus Christ, she's so sexy.

Sometimes I can't believe she's real.

My dick stirs again at the sight of her, and I reach down to adjust it through my jeans, gritting my teeth at Trystan when I realize he's watching *my* girl, not his own.

"The fuck are you looking at?"

"That smile on her face," he answers, throwing me a knowing grin over his shoulder as he walks toward Andie. "I haven't seen it in seven months."

My shoulders drop, and my lips curve into my own smile as I think about his words.

That smile's because of me.

Just as I take a step closer to her, some high school senior I vaguely recognize bumps right into her side, too drunk to watch where he's going, the fucking idiot. He turns around fast and grabs her waist to stop her from falling over, his eyes widening when he gets a good look at the smoking hot girl he's touching. She pushes his hands away from her, and he does take a step back, but then he gives her body a slow once-over, and now I'm going to kill him. I see red and smash one of the empty beer bottles on the bar, walking over to the little shit and shoving him back a few steps, away from Violet.

"You stupid motherfucker." I seethe in his face, holding the broken bottle up to his cheek, but before I can start beating the shit out of him, I'm yanked back by my arms, and my wrists are suddenly locked behind my back. "Tryst—"

"Atticus, don't!" Andie shouts at me, quickly stepping between me and the kid with her hands up, eyes wide as she drills them into mine. "*Don't.*"

I growl and twist in Trystan's grip, feeling him snatch the neck of the bottle and throw it down on the ground. "Why the fuck do you care if I hit him?"

"We're not stopping you for him, you idiot." She steps into me, bravely snatching my jaw to twist my head to the right. "We're stopping you for *you*."

My vision tunnels, and I give up fighting them when I realize she's making me look at Violet. She's leaning back against the bar with her legs crossed at the ankle, casually sipping from the bottle of tequila I got for her, the expression on her face giving absolutely nothing away. She's just *staring* at me, waiting for me to make my choice.

Goddamnit.

Trystan slowly uncurls his fingers from around my

wrists, like he's unsure whether he should let me go or not. I shake him off and move around to the guy I'm not killing, my heart still racing as I grip the front of his shirt and pull him into me.

"You're so fucking lucky I love her too much to throw you into that fire," I say quietly, tilting my head in Violet's direction to make sure he knows exactly who I'm talking about. "Don't touch my girl. Don't look at my girl. Don't even walk by her. You hear me?"

He swallows and nods, and I release him with a shove, resisting the urge to shove my fist into his face, just once. Knowing *I'll* be the dead one if I do that, I walk over to Violet and place both hands on the bar on either side of her, really struggling not to lose my shit.

Fuck, this is killing me.

Her mouth tips up at the side, and she takes another sip of her drink before setting it down behind her. "That was really hard for you, wasn't it?" she asks, looking down at my body as she runs her cold fingertips over my chest and abs.

"It's not funny," I breathe out, clutching her forearms and dropping my forehead to hers. "I think I'm having a panic attack."

She chuckles and slides her hands up to my neck, running her nails through my hair to calm me down, to restrain me the way only she can. I kiss her and force my tongue into her mouth, claiming her for every motherfucker to see, driving my point home.

Mine, mine, mine.

"Baby, tell me yes."

"I'm telling you maybe."

I huff through my nose and tilt my face down to her neck. Kissing her throbbing pulse, I discreetly move one hand down beneath her skirt, over her pussy until I find the plug in her ass, pushing on it and twisting it, making her squirm and wiggle against me.

"I need to taste you again."

"Right here?"

"*No*," I growl, making her laugh.

She reaches around for the tequila and brings it with her, locking our fingers together and pulling me back into the darkness of the woods.

"Slower," she demands, pushing down on my head to set the pace she wants.

I'm on my knees for her like the good boyfriend I am, her back pressed up against a tree with her legs spread wide open, the right one locked over my shoulder. All she's wearing is her boots and my t-shirt, clutching the hem at her ribs so she can watch what I'm doing to her. That tight leather skirt of hers was getting in my way, so I got rid of it somewhere about a half a mile back, much to her annoyance, but she's not complaining now.

Slowing down a bit, I spread her pussy with my thumbs and lick around her lips, then down to her entrance before I slide back up to her clit. "You want me to tease you?"

"Mhmm," she moans, scrunching her eyes shut with her mouth parted. "Fuck."

"Eyes open, Vi," I remind her. "Keep looking at me."

Once she's looking down at me again, I hold her stare and gently flick her clit with my tongue, over and over and over again. Her hips buck and she rolls them into me, trying to get more, so I slide two fingers up her inner thigh and push them inside her, twisting them around and nudging the plug in her ass. I manage to fit a third one in, and she moans louder, yanking my head back by my hair. Knowing exactly how to set her off, I stick my tongue all the way out for her so she can rub herself on it, groaning at the taste of us both sliding down my throat. I don't usually swallow my own cum, but I know it drives her wild to watch me eat it out of her, and I fucking love how rough she gets with me when I do it.

Just as her legs start to clamp around my head, I seal my mouth over her pussy and suck on her clit, curling my fingers into her faster and harder. "You ready to come for me?"

"Fuck. *Yes*."

"Good girl," I rasp, squeezing her ass and spreading her cheeks, ensuring she feels the effects of the plug. "Pull my hair again and come all over my face."

"Fuck," she says again. "Fuck, Atty…"

Doing exactly as I told her to, she grinds herself on me and fucks my mouth, sliding herself up and down until she's shaking and jerking against me. Her knees give out before she's even finished, and I catch her in my lap, easing my fingers in and out of her to coax her through it. She pushes my hand away once she's had enough, breathing hard against my face with her arms around my neck and her forehead leaning on mine.

"You're filthy, you know that?" she asks, moving to clean the wetness from my lips.

I grab her hand before she can, pulling her mouth to mine and forcing her to taste herself. I lick my tongue over hers, and she kisses me back without argument, falling down on me as we make out like we used to when we were fourteen, making my dick leak inside my boxers. I rub it on her through my jeans, and she pulls back and looks down at her pussy, hissing at how used and sensitive it must feel.

"We're not done yet, are we?" she asks, sighing when I smirk up at her.

"If you have to ask me that," I tease, rolling her onto her side and pulling her shirt back up, dipping my head to get to her nipples. "Baby, you don't know me at all."

CHAPTER 10
VIOLET

I'm back in Atticus's lap and laughing so hard my insides hurt, munching on the strawberry ice cream we got from the gas station a little while ago. We walked there and back after he fucked me for the fifth time…or maybe it was the sixth. I stopped keeping count hours ago. I don't know what time it is now, but I really don't care. I'm just enjoying being with him, having him back in my life after going so long without him.

"Didn't he puke after like two minutes?" I ask as I look up, remembering the time in sophomore year when he strung his older brother up to the huge tree we're sitting under by his ankles, all because he hugged me hello at their house one time.

He nods and feeds me another fingerful of ice cream, grinning as he licks some off his knuckles. "Phoenix made me cut him down before he choked and died up there."

I laugh harder and reach over to run my fingertips over the letters we carved into this very tree a few years ago. *AL & VS*—our initials written inside the shape of a heart, of course, because we were *so* cool and hopelessly in love back in high school.

"I love you, Atty," I breathe out, dropping my head to kiss his nose, making him smile.

"Are you still stoned?"

"And drunk," I add, picking up the tequila to uncap it, pouting when he takes it away from me.

"No more," he says, hiding it behind him.

"Why not?"

"Because I'm not ready for you to pass out yet."

I hum on a long exhale and take the tub of ice cream he's holding instead, scooping some out and holding it up for him, not surprised when he scrunches his nose at me.

"It's so weird you don't like ice cream."

"It's cold."

"Want me to warm it up for you?" I ask playfully, licking it off my finger and swirling it around with my tongue, enjoying the heated look in his eyes.

Taking his jaw, I open his mouth and press mine to his, kissing him and feeding him the melted ice cream. A bit drips out of the corner of his mouth, and I dip my head to catch it, licking up his throat and back to his lips.

I tug on the bottom one with my teeth, pushing myself down on the hardness I can feel poking into me beneath his jeans. That really gets him going, and then he's pulling back to devour my body with his eyes.

"Bend over so I can see your pussy and ass together."

I quickly obey and get myself into position, placing my knees either side of his thighs so I can push my hips back into him. After spreading me open with his thumbs, he doesn't do anything for a minute. He just *stares*, and I'm getting impatient. But then I feel something cold and wet dripping over my pussy, and I gasp when he pushes his face against me and licks the ice cream off my clit. He gently takes the plug out of my ass, and it makes me cry out when he licks me there too.

Fuck.

Fuck, that's so damn dirty, but it feels *so* damn good.

"Listen to you, moaning for it like a needy little slut," he says, rolling the tip of his cold tongue over my hole. "You like it when I eat this pretty ass?"

I nod, and he keeps going, fucking his fingers into my pussy at the same time. Still holding the toy, he moves it back to my hole and uses it to open me up more, pausing every few seconds to come at me with his tongue again.

"Atty…"

"Is it ready for me?" he asks, his low voice vibrating against my flesh.

I nod again, knowing this was coming. He loves

fucking me there, not just because of how tight he says it is, but because he knows I love it just as much. I don't know what it is about having his dick in my ass, especially from this angle, but it drives me crazy every time.

I feel him move, and then his thighs are pressed against the backs of mine, his left hand holding my hip as he uses the other one to tease me with the tip of his cock. He spits on us both before he pushes it in so slowly—so slowly I could kill him. I tell myself to breathe and curl my nails into the dirt beneath me, waiting for more. He gives it to me, and then he's finally all the way inside, and I can feel every hard inch of him in my ass.

"*Fuck.*"

"You okay?"

"Yeah," I say on a whimper, already feeling myself clenching around him. "Atty, move."

"I think you should beg me again," he taunts. "You look so pretty when you beg."

"I will stab you in your sleep," I grit out, making him laugh.

He pulls out about an inch before fucking it back in, gently at first, and then he sets a steady pace and really gets going. His hands are all over me, roughly grabbing my waist, my thighs, my ass. I know he's doing it just so he can see the bruises on me tomorrow, but I don't care. I'm fully aware how twisted it is, but I want that just as much as he does. I want him to make me feel him for days after we're done here.

Pushing myself up from my hands and knees, I press my back to his front and take his hand, placing it between my breasts and moving it up to my neck. He hesitates, just for a second, and then he tightens his grip and pulls my head back on his shoulder.

"You want me to choke you, dirty girl?" he asks in my ear, his barely there control slipping.

"Make it hurt a bit."

He growls out a curse and twists the chain I'm wearing between his fingers. With one hand clutching my stomach, he squeezes my throat with his necklace until I can feel the pendant biting at my flesh. Turning my face, he takes my lip between his teeth and bites down on it, not letting up when I cry out over his mouth.

"You're fucking perfect," he says. "You were fucking *made* for me, Violet."

I breathe in as much air as he's allowing me and nod, my eyes rolling back when he reaches down to play with my pussy. It's awkward at this angle, but he makes it work, hooking his fingers inside me before he pulls them out and rubs them over my clit.

"Oh shit," I croak, voice raspy from being strangled. "Atty, you're gonna make me come."

He chokes me harder until I can't see anything in front of me anymore. All I can do is *feel* as he fucks his cock into me and pushes me over the edge.

"God, I love your ass," he groans, and then he's

coming too, locking his arm around my middle so hard I'm sure he's trying to crush me to death. *"Fuck…"*

I cough and splutter, and he stills before he finally lets me go. I fall forward and catch myself on my hands, feeling his eyes on me as he pulls out and watches him cum drip out of my hole and down to my pussy. He mutters something I don't catch, and I drop my face to my forearms, ready to fall asleep right here with my bare ass in the air.

"Baby," he says, loud enough for me to hear it this time. "You still with me?"

"I don't know *where* the fuck I am, Atty."

He chuckles and carefully picks me up to turn me around. He pulls his shirt back down to cover my thighs, and I lie on the ground with a grimace, suddenly hurting all over. Our knees are raw and my lip feels like it's swollen where he bit me, but I don't even bother pretending to be pissed about it. I just close my eyes and curl up into his side, smiling to myself at his familiar warmth and his scent wrapped around me.

The way it's supposed to be…

CHAPTER 11
ATTICUS

She's so fucking beautiful in the light of day.

The sun came up a little while ago, lighting the right side of her pale face and allowing me to really *see* her for the first time since I was locked up. Phoenix sent me a picture of her to keep in my cell after I threatened to kill him on day five, but nothing will ever be as good as the real thing. She looks like a dark, fallen angel sent just for me. Lying on her side with her head on my arm, her hands tucked under her chin to keep them warm, her long eyelash extensions fluttering every now and again as she breathes in and out through her nose.

Unable to help myself, I lift my hand up to her face and tuck her hair behind her ear, recounting the black and purple piercings there. She got another one while I was in jail—another little black ring on the top part of her outer ear, making it ten piercings total just here—but that's the only thing that's different about her body. She doesn't have any new ink or anything else I don't know about. I know because I've been searching. For the last hour, maybe more, I've been lying here with my girl in my arms and investigating every inch of her body, dying for her to wake up because I fucking miss her already.

I sigh and move my hand down to hers, watching her face while I lift it up to my mouth and kiss my name tattooed on the inside of her wrist. She finally stirs after what feels like years, and I grin as she cracks one eye open to look over at me.

"Fucking hell," she croaks out, clearing her throat as she tries to lift her head, turning it slowly to take in our surroundings. "I don't miss this part. Being with you. I forgot how much it hurts waking up in strange places with a fucked up back."

"I'll fix it," I say eagerly, sitting up to massage it for her, rubbing the life back into her sore muscles. "I'll fix *everything*, Vi. I'm gonna make it all better. You'll see."

Instead of responding, she lies flat on her stomach and rests her cheek on her folded hands, simply enjoying the attention I'm giving her.

"You still love me when you're sober?"

She opens one eye again and scrunches her face up, hesitating as if she has to think about it. "I don't think I'm sober yet," she finally says. "Ask me later."

"I'm asking now."

She sighs and lifts herself up on her forearms, meeting my gaze over her shoulder. "I *do* love you. But I don't know if I can…" she trails off, studying me for my reaction. "What if we're only together on Joker Night? I can meet you right here every year and—" She stops talking altogether then, frowning at the glare on my face. "What?"

"You're joking, right?"

She grins like the evil little brat she is, and I lunge for her, chasing her when she squeals and jumps up to run away from me. *Again.* But I don't let her get very far this time, catching her after just a few seconds and lifting her up by her waist.

"Don't carry me."

"I'll do whatever the fuck I want with you." I spin her around, hauling her ass up and wrapping her legs around my waist. "And you'll like it."

She growls and tilts my face up by my jaw, but I can tell she's trying not to smile. "Fine," she says, acting as if she's not as happy about this as I am. "But can you at least *try* to be a better person so I don't have to defend you to my parents every time you fuck up?"

"Fine."

"You'll stop acting like a psycho and trying to kill anyone who looks at me?"

"No," I answer. "But I promise I won't get caught again."

She rolls her eyes and wraps her arms around my

neck, hiding her big grin on my shoulder while I walk her back toward the main road.

"Want me to take you for breakfast at Lucky's?"

"Is that even a question?"

I chuckle and set her down on her feet next to Phoenix's car. He let me drive here last night and I still have the keys in my pocket. I unlock it and open the back door, searching the mess in here to grab myself a t-shirt to wear. I don't want Violet wearing his shit, but she's shivering her little ass off, and I'm not about to let her freeze to death. I reluctantly pass her the cleanest hoodie I can find, and she throws it on, shaking her head at me with a snort when she catches the way my teeth mesh together.

"I'll buy you a new one from that store opposite the diner."

"Of course you will," she jokes, pulling the hem down to her thighs.

I leave Phoenix's keys on the front tire for him, and then the two of us start walking along the side of the road hand in hand.

"Where's my car?" I ask, because neither it nor the keys were at the apartment when I went there to snoop through her stuff yesterday.

"Andie's house."

"You drove it while I was gone?"

"At least once every two days."

"Did you—"

"Wait for it to heat up first every time?" she finishes for me. "Yes, Atty."

"Good girl," I praise, lifting her hand up to my mouth to kiss her knuckles.

"I also took it to your guy for an oil change last month and never let the gas run below a quarter full," she adds, looking awfully proud of herself when I let out a low groan.

"I wanna marry you so bad."

"Oh yeah?"

"Let's go to Vegas and elope later."

"Ha." She laughs. "One step a time, baby."

"You wanna have kids first?"

Her eyes widen as she suddenly stops, and I curse myself for opening my big mouth.

"We're going to the pharmacy. Right now," she decides, picking up the pace and dragging me along by my wrist. "I'll call the doctor tomorrow morning so she can get me back on the pill," she goes on, turning around to point a finger at my face. "*You* better stay the fuck out of my medicine cabinet."

I nod fast, a little scared of her when she looks at me like that. "All right."

After we've been to the pharmacy and the clothing store across the street—in that order, as she insisted—I finally manage to get some chocolate chip pancakes into her at Lucky's Diner. She looks so fucking cute wearing the huge gray hoodie I bought her, using the sleeves to hold her steaming hot coffee cup as she sips it in the booth seat next to me.

"We don't know if anyone found the Joker card," she says, eyeing me over the top.

"Don't even worry about it," I tell her, shaking my head. "There's no way."

She nods her agreement and tucks her feet up on my lap, raising a brow at me when I continue to play with this new piercing in her ear, brushing my thumb over the metal.

"When did you get this?" I ask, because I've been dying to know since I found it on her this morning.

She shrugs, hesitating before she says, "I don't rememb—"

"Violet."

"April seventh."

My court date.

That shouldn't please me as much as it does, but I can't help it.

Back in high school, every time she'd get into yet another screaming fight with her parents—usually about me—or whenever she'd feel anxious or stressed or sad about something, she'd call me to come get her and I'd take her to get something new for her body. New ink or a new piercing. It's why she's covered in them. They always make her feel better about whatever's tearing her up inside at the time.

And she got this on my court date.

She hits me with a small, half smile, and I smile too, dropping my head down on her shoulder and tightening my grip around her waist. "You went without me," I say into her hoodie, moving my mouth up to kiss the shell of her ear.

"One time," she mutters. "It's just a teeny little ring, Atty."

"You got a girl to do it, right?"

"Fucking hell."

"What?" I ask. "I'm just curious."

She sighs heavily and goes back to her coffee, not saying anything else about it. She didn't actually answer my question, but I'm not worried. She knows damn well if I found out she let another guy put hands on her, I'd find him and cut his fucking dick off.

Just as I'm picturing it, the dipshit waiter approaches us *again*, bouncing his eyes between us both as if he's never seen two people covered in paint and dirt and bruises before. I set Violet's coffee down on the table and turn her face toward mine, kissing her right in front of him because I can't not do it. It's just a natural instinct for me—this *need* I have to claim and own and protect her.

"I'll be good," I say quietly, and she lets out one of those sexy little laughs I love so much, her lips moving against mine.

"As if you know the meaning of the word."

"Can I get you anything else?" the guy interrupts us, nervously shifting from foot to foot, and I swear to God I'm not imagining the way he keeps trying to make eye contact with Violet, like he thinks she's a hostage who needs saving from me or some shit.

As if this scrawny fucker thinks he could do anything about it.

When I do nothing but sit here and stare him out, silently daring him to look at her again, Violet takes pity on the guy and puts him out of his misery. "Just the check, please."

He scurries off with a nod, and I kiss her one more time, running my fingers through her hair as I relax back into my seat and look toward the main door. It's busy in here this morning, just like it is every Sunday, the staff running around like crazy trying to get everybody their food. I recognize a few people and a couple of the kids from the party last night, but none of our friends have shown up like they usually do the morning after.

"Where is everyone?"

"Fuck knows where Tryst and Andie are," Violet answers with a knowing little smirk, dipping her finger into the leftover syrup on her plate and licking it off. "I haven't seen Nova since she bailed on us last night. And I didn't see Phoenix at all."

I blink at hearing my twin sister's name. I haven't really thought about her since I've been back—I've been too focused on Violet—but now that Vi mentions her...

"Nova was at the party?" I ask, and she nods as she swallows another sip of her coffee.

"We picked her up on the way, but she disappeared as soon as we got there."

My brows dip, and I take the new phone I bought yesterday out of my back pocket, tapping her number and pressing it to my ear. She doesn't pick up the first time, or the second, so I keep trying, losing patience and bouncing my knee beneath the table.

"Jesus, *what*?" she finally answers, like the loving little shit she is.

"Where the fuck are you?"

"None of your *fucking* business."

I raise a brow at that, chuckling to myself when I realize she's perfectly fine. "Don't you wanna see me now I'm home?"

"Not really."

I'm about to say more, but then she hangs up on me, and I pull the phone away from my ear to frown at it. "Bitch."

Violet laughs into her mug, and I wait for her to

finish the rest, tossing some cash down once she's done and pulling her up to stand.

"Let's go."

"Where?" she asks, wiping her mouth with the back of her hand.

"I wanna fuck you again before I drive you home."

CHAPTER 12
VIOLET

By the time we get to Atticus's mom's house, I'm dead on my feet and in desperate need of a hot shower. I'm pretty sure he's thinking the same thing, but not to get ourselves clean. He's got that look in his eye—the one that says he wants to dirty me up again.

No one answers the front door when he knocks, so he takes me around the porch to the back of the house, urging me to climb through the open kitchen window.

"You gotta be kidding me," I whisper-yell. "Atty, that window is tiny."

"So are you."

I huff and place my hands on his shoulders, allowing him to boost me up so I can break into his poor mother's house. This makes no sense, considering we could just go back to Andie's, pick up his car and drive to a hotel or something, but I don't bother arguing with him over it. Maybe he just wants to spend some time in his childhood home after being away for so long. Or maybe he's just horny and doesn't want to wait a minute longer.

It's probably the second one.

I have to step on the white countertop to get in, so I quickly hop down to the floor and grab a towel to clean the mess I made, laughing at the impatient look Atticus is giving me from outside. Taking off my filthy boots, I carry them through the house and meet him at the front door, unlocking it for him and letting him inside. I put my shoes down on the mat, and he watches what I'm doing, kicking his off too before he comes right for me.

It doesn't sound like anyone's home, but I don't think he gives a shit either way. He'd fuck me right here on the floor in the entryway if I asked him to.

He grabs my waist, and our mouths meet in a filthy kiss as he walks us toward the curved staircase. We get up to the first floor, almost tripping as we go, and he takes me along the hall to his bedroom—the same one we had sex in for the first time back in high school. I've only ever been with him, and he's only ever been with me. It's *always* been just us, ever since we were old enough to realize we were more than just childhood friends.

"What do you think your mom's gonna say when she finds out we're back together?"

"I don't care," he answers, nipping at my swollen lip.

"My mom's gonna lose her shit," I mutter into his mouth. "And my dad…"

"*I don't care.*" He says it slower this time, breaking the kiss to look me in the eye. "You're mine and I'm yours, Vi. Fucking simple. Nothing anyone says or does to us is ever gonna change that. *You* couldn't even change it. Our fucking parents don't stand a chance."

I nod because he's right, then I wrap my hands around his neck and pull him down to me. He backs me up into his and Nova's old bathroom and guides me to the shower, turning the water on before pulling my hoodie over my head. He rids me of his t-shirt next, and I do a double take when I catch my own reflection in the mirror.

"*Shit,*" I hiss, taking a step closer to get a better look at my naked body.

I knew it was gonna be bad, but I didn't expect it to be *this* bad. I'm covered in cuts and bruises—small fingertip-shaped ones on my throat, my hips, my thighs, my ass. My lip is bruised too, and I don't even wanna count the hickeys on my chest, neck, and jaw.

My fucking *jaw*.

"Jesus, Atty. Have you seen the state of me?"

"I can't stop looking," he murmurs, pulling me back by my hand.

"How am I supposed to go to school like this?"

"Take a week off."

"I'm a pre-law student, you dick," I bite out,

choosing not to disclose the fact that I've been ditching class for months now. "I can't just—"

"Shh," he whispers, guiding me into the walk-in shower. "Stop complaining when we both know you love it almost as much as I do."

I grit my teeth and look away, shaking my head with a grin.

This cocky prick.

He strips out of his clothes and steps into the shower with me, walking me forward into the stream of water. It stings a little when it hits the cuts, but only for a few seconds. After the initial burn wears off, the hot water starts to feel amazing on my skin, and so do his hands, rubbing my sore neck and shoulders from behind.

He tips my head back and wets my hair, then grabs the shampoo, washing and rinsing it before he runs the coconut scented conditioner through it. My hair is heavy when it's soaking wet because it's so long and thick, so he gathers it all in one hand, holding it up at the back of my head to take the weight off for me. I sigh happily and lean back into his warm body, closing my eyes and turning my face into his chest.

"I missed you so much, Atty."

"I know you did, baby girl," he says softly. "I missed you too."

Pumping some of his shower gel into his free hand—the same one his mom's been stocking for him here even after we left for college two years ago—he soaps me up and gently washes my breasts, my stomach, and then finally my pussy. I gasp at the feel of his fingers sliding over my lips, his hard dick poking the top of my ass from behind. I push myself back into it, and he growls, tightening his grip on my pussy to keep me still.

"Not yet," he says, pumping some more shower gel to wash his own body.

He's a lot rougher with himself, still holding my hair with one hand as he lathers up his cock to get it nice and clean for me. He pulls back a bit to rinse off, and then I'm suddenly pushed up against the black-tiled wall, shivering at how cold it is against my breasts and stomach. His grip on my hair turns painful, and he uses it to keep me right where he wants me, kicking my legs apart before he nudges himself up to my pussy. He pauses for a second, and I go still too, looking back to try to figure out what stopped him.

"I love it when you smell like me." He tilts my head to the side and presses his nose to the crook of my neck, inhaling me with a groan. "Get up on your tiptoes."

He pushes in, and my hands slip on the wall without anything to hold on to. Instead of moving right away, he keeps himself buried inside me and just breathes me in.

"Promise you'll never try to leave me again."

"I promise."

"Good," he says. "Because I won't let you off this easy next time." His other hand comes up to grab both of my arms, and he folds them behind me at the bottom of my back, making me slip even more. "I'll lock you up if I have to, Vi. I'll sew my fucking skin to yours. You won't get away from me."

"Atty."

"Yes, baby?"

"Shut up and fuck me."

He laughs cruelly before he does as I say, fucking me hard into the wall, kissing my jaw and nipping it with his teeth, claiming me and hurting me all at once.

This is what he loves—ruining me, fixing me back up, and then ruining me all over again.

And something tells me that after what I did to him, he's only just getting started.

The End

ACKNOWLEDGMENTS

To my brother-in-law, Keiron. You know why <3

To my husband and son, and our beautiful family and friends, thanks for everything you do for me. You're the BEST support system and I love you all so much. But please don't read my books. Lol!

To Corina Ciobanu, my amazing assistant, alpha reader, one of the best friends I've ever had and the person I run to when the sky is falling. What would I do without you? I'd crash and burn. Thank you for keeping me sane(ish). Love you, C.

To my beta readers and book besties: Mari Silva, the sweetest little baddie I've ever known, and Xander Beck, my stabby, unhinged, chaotic guy. I'm so freaking lucky to have you crazy two in my corner. I love you both.

To Ria from Graphic Escapist, thank you so much for this BEAUTIFUL cover. I still can't stop staring at it.

To my editor, Zainab M, who edited this entire thing for me from her hospital bed. Dude, you're a freaking rockstar. Thanks for giving a shit about my shit. You were made for me and I'm keeping you forever. Or maybe you're keeping me. That sounds more like it.

To my proofreader, Amber Nicole, thanks for smashing this out on top of everything else you've got going on. You're the best.

To my ARC Team and Street Team, thank you so much for all the early feedback, the stunning edits and reviews and everything else you all do for me.

To Cat, Jessica, Rebecca, and all the bloggers at JLRC Author services, thank you for everything.

To everyone in Bethany Winters' Book Baddies, you guys are my home and I couldn't do this without you.

And to every single person who read this book, thanks for taking a chance on me and my story.

All my love,
Bethany <3

ALSO BY BETHANY WINTERS

The Kingston Brothers Series

Kings of Westbrook High

Reckless at Westbrook High

Chaos at Westbrook High (Coming Soon)

Standalones

Little Devil

Dirty Love

ABOUT THE AUTHOR

Bethany lives in South Wales with her husband and their six year old son. Her favourite things are books, tea, oversized hoodies, and Machine Gun Kelly, although her husband is still pretty mad about that last one. When she's not writing, she's either daydreaming about all the crazy characters inside her head, reading, or raiding Amazon for pretty paperbacks to hoard.

Join Bethany Winters' Book Baddies to be the first to know about anything and everything Bethany related.

Sign up for her newsletter to receive (irregular) updates on what she's reading and writing about, early teasers, new releases, bonus scenes, giveaways, and more: https://bethanywinters.co.uk/subscribe

Manufactured by Amazon.ca
Bolton, ON